For Fitzy–
May you always love animals.
May you always love to read.
And may you never hear a fart
that doesn't make you laugh.

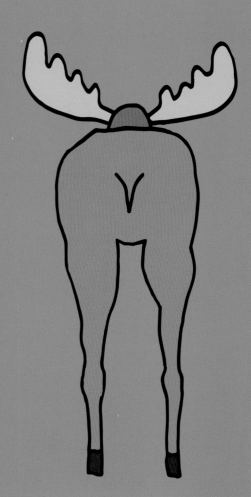

WHO FARTED?

By

Captain Jack

THE SNAKE!

You are snowshoeing through the arctic when you hear...
ART ART...FRRRPPP!!

WHO FARTED?!

You are raking leaves when you hear...Gobble Gobble...
FRRRPPP!!

WHO FARTED?!

THE TURKEY!

THE DUCKS!

You are climbing a tree in the jungle when you hear...
OOH OOH AH AH...FRRRPPP!!

WHO FARTED?!

THE MONKEY!

THE TYRANNOSAURUS REX!

You are reading a book when you hear.......... FRRRRRPPP!!!!

WHO FARTED?!

YOU
FARTED!!